# USBORNE PUZZLE ADVENTURES
## The Missing Unicorn

Russell Punter

Illustrated by Fabiano Fiorin

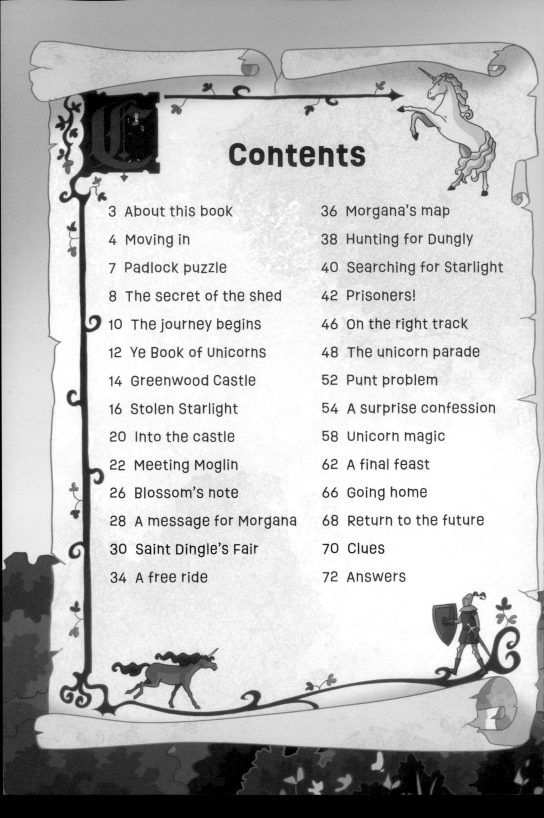

# Contents

3 About this book

4 Moving in

7 Padlock puzzle

8 The secret of the shed

10 The journey begins

12 Ye Book of Unicorns

14 Greenwood Castle

16 Stolen Starlight

20 Into the castle

22 Meeting Moglin

26 Blossom's note

28 A message for Morgana

30 Saint Dingle's Fair

34 A free ride

36 Morgana's map

38 Hunting for Dungly

40 Searching for Starlight

42 Prisoners!

46 On the right track

48 The unicorn parade

52 Punt problem

54 A surprise confession

58 Unicorn magic

62 A final feast

66 Going home

68 Return to the future

70 Clues

72 Answers

# About this book

The **Missing Unicorn** will whirl you back to a time of kings and castles, in search of a magical unicorn.

Throughout the book, there are lots of puzzles and brain-teasing problems to solve.

Study the pictures and look out for vital clues and information. Sometimes you'll need to flick back through the book to find an answer.

Don't worry if you can't solve every puzzle — some are trickier than others!

There are extra clues to help you on pages 70 to 71 and you can check the answers on pages 72 to 79.

# Moving in

It was a big day for Jade. She had just moved into her Auntie Blossom's rambling old house.

The rooms were full of crates, not to mention her grumpy parents, so she was off to explore the garden...

Let's see what's in this shed, Leo!

WOOF!

# Padlock puzzle

"**D**id you know my Auntie Blossom?" asked Jade. "She used to live here."

Jack shook his head.

"She was an explorer," Jade added, "and she went all over the world."

Leo began pawing at the shed door.

"I was about to look in here," Jade examined the shed padlock, "but this needs three numbers to unlock it. My auntie loved puzzles and codes. If only she'd left the numbers written down somewhere."

Jack read the top sign on the shed out loud. "I think she did!" he said.

**Can you work out the three numbers?**

Don't forget to lock the gate.

Keep out!

I ♥ my shed

# The secret of the shed

The door creaked open...
"So much stuff!" gasped Jade.

"Maybe your aunt collected it on her travels," said Jack.

"Maybe," Jade agreed. "But lots of these things look hundreds of years old."

"They must have been really expensive," said Jack. "Was your aunt super rich?"

"Not at all." Jade frowned. "And have you noticed? Every single thing looks brand new!"

Queen Morgana
Reign: 1375-1405

REMINDER
–DO NOT TOUCH UNLESS
PREPARED TO TRAVEL!

Queen Victoria
Born: 1819
Died: 1901

Jack pointed to a black and white photograph in a gold frame. One of the women in the photo looked a little like Jade. "Hey, is this your aunt?"

Jade looked at the photo. It *was* her auntie, beside a white-haired lady who looked familiar. "Yes that's her, when she was about thirty, I'd guess," replied Jade, as she studied the faces. "But something about this picture can't be right!"

**What has Jade spotted?**

# The journey begins

After Jade has explained her idea to Jack...

But that's **crazy**! How could your aunt be around in the 1890s?

By now, she'd have been around... **150** years old!

I know. Unless...

Careful, *Leo!*

THUD!

Hey, this book feels kind of... fizzy!

I hope it doesn't have mites... or weevils!

# Ye Book of Unicorns

The next thing they knew, Jade, Jack and Leo were lying on the ground in a moonlit forest.

"Where are we?" said Jack, scrambling to his feet. "And WHAT AM I WEARING?!"

"No idea," said Jade. "But I think it has something to do with this book."

"*Ye Book of Unicorns*," read Jack. "Maybe if we touch it again, it'll send us back." He tapped the book cautiously. Nothing. "Looks like we're stuck here," he sighed. "Wherever **here** is..."

Jade flicked through the book hoping it would give some answers. "Ah," she said, looking at a page about four unicorns. "I know exactly where we are!"

**Do you?**

## Ye Isle of Myrtle Unicorn

*Only found on the Isle of Myrtle off the northwest coast. This unicorn is said to be so tame that it can be ridden.*

## Ye Crag Mountain Unicorn

*Inhabits the high mountain ranges of the kingdom. Rarely seen, as its white coat makes it hard to spot against the snow.*

## Ye Greenwood Unicorn

*Lives in the royal stables at Greenwood Castle close to Greenwood Forest. Eats the blue-leafed clover that only grows in Greenwood Forest.*

## Ye Heather Valley Unicorn

*Easily made out against the slopes of pink heather. Many have tried to tame the creature, but none have succeeded.*

# Greenwood Castle

"If we're in Greenwood Forest, then the castle is nearby," said Jade. "We can ask for help."

Jack shrugged. "But that book *also* says unicorns are **real**... We must be miles from anywhere. Now I don't even have my phone to check."

They had only walked for a few minutes when a vast castle came into view.

"There must be someone at home," said Jade. "Let's go in and see."

GRIFFIN GATE

GRIFFIN GATE

As they were crossing the drawbridge, a cart shot past. Jade and Jack leaped out of the way and fell into the moat.

"Road hog!" spluttered Jade, as the cart disappeared.

They swam to the edge of the moat and clambered out of the ice-cold, filthy water, their teeth chattering.

"L-l-look at this," said Jade, picking up a scrap of paper from the bridge. "F-f-fell from the cart."

"It's n-n-nonsense," said Jack, spitting out mud.

"At first glance," agreed Jade."But try reading downwards instead of across!"

Take the magic of the wonderful unicorn for example – at its best at midnight or midday. All you need is to be prepared for wonder.

**What does the message say?**

# Stolen Starlight

As Jack and Jade enter the courtyard...

**Starlight**! Have you seen Starlight?

Who's that, your cat?

No, *Starlight*, King Edgar's unicorn, of course!

King? Unicorn?!

We haven't actually *seen* it. But we did find this note...

Jade explains about the note...

Oh no! Starlight's been **stolen** and it's all my fault!

Who are you?

I'm the squire, Tom. But who are **you**, and why are you so wet?

We fell in the mo— *Achoo!*

You'd better come into the stables and warm yourselves.

Do you have a phone we can use to call our parents?

What's a *phone*?

This may seem a silly question, Tom, but what year is it?

1375 of course!

**1375**! Are you crazy?

Sorry, Tom. Jack isn't very good on dates.

Well at least I haven't lost a unicorn!

What exactly happened, Tom?

I arrived to spend the night in the stables, as usual.

I'd just finished my evening drink from the kitchens, when I suddenly felt very sleepy.

When I woke up, Starlight had gone!

# Into the castle

"**B**ut Moglin wrote the label on *that* bottle!" said Tom. "He's the king's wise man — and he's my *friend*. He'd never give me a sleeping potion."

"Perhaps someone stole it from him," suggested Jack.

"If your friend Moglin is as wise as you say, he might be able to help you find Starlight," said Jade.
"You're right!" said Tom. "Let's go to his chambers."

As Tom led them through the silent castle, Jack whispered urgently to Jade. "How did we end up *here*? And *how* are we going to get back?"

Jade and Jack are here.

"I think my auntie could travel in time," Jade murmured in reply. "If *she* got home again, so can we."

Leo barked excitedly as a rat scuttled past, and raced after it. "Leo! Come back!" hissed Jade.

"I'll find him," said Tom. "You go on to Moglin's chambers. Just take the first turn after the second blue torch, past the Greenwood Unicorn tapestry, turn left, then right and it's the second arched door with the red and green griffin."

**Which is the door to Moglin's chambers?**

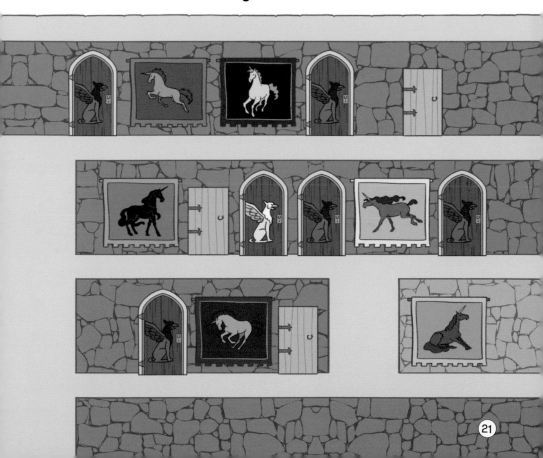

# Meeting Moglin

Tom soon returns with Leo. He knocks on Moglin's door and shows them inside...

Wow!

What an amazing room!

I suppose these are Moglin's potions.

Don't drink **that**, whatever you do!

Moglin!

Er, sorry. Is it deadly poison?

Certainly not! It's my last bottle of prune and turnip wine!

Tom introduces his new friends and tells Moglin what's happened...

Starlight? Stolen? That's **terrible**! Especially now.

Why?

23

Moglin mutters some magic words and...

**Who stole the sleeping potion?**

# Blossom's note

**"I**'m not surprised," said Tom. "Morgana's the king's sister and she's thoroughly wicked."

"But why steal the unicorn?" asked Jack.

Moglin frowned. "Without Starlight's powers, the king may die and then Morgana will be queen!"

Jade thought back to the note that fell from the cart. "Morgana may have put the potion in Tom's drink. But someone else took Starlight out of the castle."

"Probably Morgana's servant, Dungly," said Tom. "He's as bad as she is."

"We can do nothing more tonight," said Moglin. "Sleep here. I'll check on the king."

"I only went into the garden to play keepy-uppy," sighed Jack, as they tried to get comfortable. "Now I'm tracking down unicorns in the Middle Ages!"

"Don't worry," said Jade. "I'm sure we'll get home somehow."

As she looked through the Book of Unicorns for any clues, a slip of paper dropped out. "That's my auntie's handwriting," she said.

Jack glanced at the odd writing. "Pity we can't read it," he said sleepily.

"I think we can," said Jade, looking around her. "We just need something to help..."

**What can Jade use to read the note?**

Time Travel Notes

– some objects have time energy

– this energy can transport you through time

– the object can return you to your own time...

...but only after a task connected with the object has been completed!

# A message for Morgana

Early the next morning, Jade and Jack were woken by Tom bringing bread and milk.

"I've been thinking," said Jade. "Let's find Morgana and follow her. She might lead us to Starlight."

No one had a better plan, so they hastily finished eating and set off.

The whole castle was bustling with activity.
"It's Saint Dingle's Day," explained Tom. "There's a fair and a feast to prepare for."

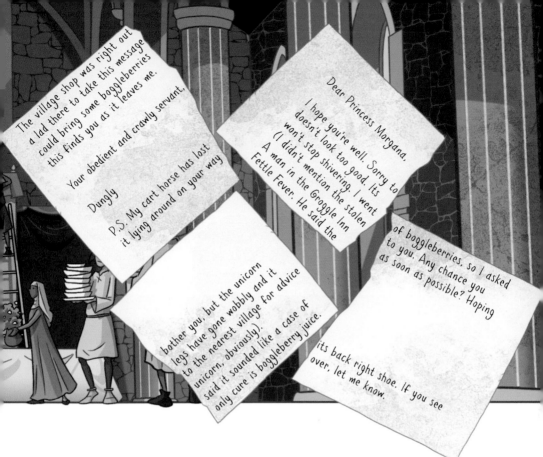

The village shop was right out
a lad there to take this message
could bring some boggleberries
this finds you as it leaves me.

Your obedient and crawly servant,

Dungly

P.S. My cart horse has lost
it lying around on your way

Dear Princess Morgana,
I hope you're well. Sorry to
doesn't look too good. Its
won't stop shivering. I went
(I didn't mention the stolen
A man in the Groggle Inn
Fettle Fever. He said the

of boggleberries, so I asked
to you. Any chance you
as soon as possible? Hoping

bother you, but the unicorn
legs have gone wobbly and it
to the nearest village for advice
unicorn, obviously).
said it sounded like a case of
only cure is boggleberry juice.

its back right shoe. If you see
over, let me know.

"Out of my way, peasants!" screeched a harsh voice, as Morgana strode through the Great Hall. "I'm taking the king's place at tonight's feast — so it had better be good!"

Just then, a boy ran up to Morgana. "A message for you, my lady," he said nervously.

Morgana snatched the note, read it, then tore it up with a snarl and stormed off. Jack quickly collected the pieces and put them together.

**What does the message say?**

# Saint Dingle's Fair

Tom led them out of the castle to where the fair was already in full swing.

"It's certainly busy!" cried Jack.

They squeezed through the crowds, looking in all directions. Jade began to feel that their search would be literally fruitless, then...

"I've seen the berry seller!" shouted Tom.

"And I've just spotted Morgana," said Jack.

**Once you've found the boggleberry seller, try and spot Morgana too.**

# A free ride

"**B**uy a few berries, Tom," said Jade. "But leave some for Morgana. Then we can follow her to Starlight."

"Good thinking," said Tom. "But we'll need horses from the stables. Starlight could be miles away."

"I'll keep an eye on Morgana while you and Jack get the horses," suggested Jade.

Tom and Jack ran back to the stables, where the castle blacksmith was hard at work.

"We need three horses, urgently," panted Tom.

"The larger chestnut is lame," said the blacksmith. "I'm halfway through putting new shoes on Dotty here. The white mare only likes female riders and the silver dappled horse next to Valiant has never been ridden."

**Which three horses can Tom and Jack take?**

Dotty    Snowflake    Molly    Valiant

# Morgana's map

Tom and Jack returned just in time to see Morgana racing by. Tom handed Jade the reins of her horse.

"Morgana has the berries," said Jade, as she popped Leo into her bag and climbed onto Snowflake.

"How do you stop this thing?" yelled Jack, galloping past on Lightning.

After a quick lesson from Tom, Jack managed to get Lightning under control and they set off.

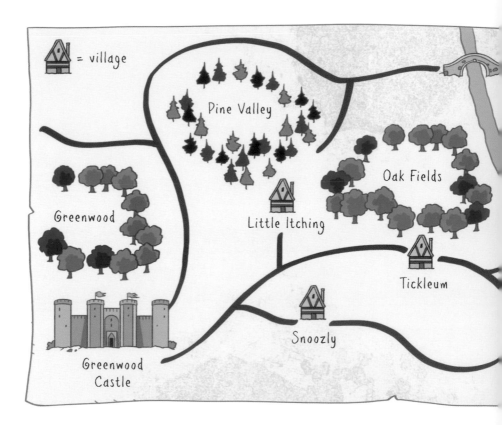

But Morgana had a more powerful horse and had soon reached a pine forest in the distance. Luckily for the three friends, in her haste, she dropped her map.

Jack thought back to Dungly's letter. It seemed Morgana was taking a route that avoided her being spotted in any villages.

"I can see a shortcut," he said. "If we take that, we should be able to catch up with her."

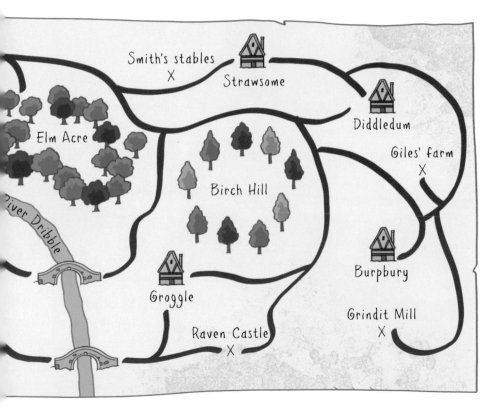

**Where is Morgana going and where is the shortcut?**

# Hunting for Dungly

The friends arrive at Groggle...

Should we wait for Morgana and follow her?

She might not come to the village.

We only know Dungly's got Starlight somewhere *near* here.

Let's ask if anyone's seen any strangers lately.

What does Dungly look like, Tom?

He's got a brown beard. He's not that tall. Oh, and he's completely bald.

Where is Dungly?

# Searching for Starlight

Jade and Jack were surprised by their first view of Raven Castle.

"It was destroyed by raiders long before I was born," explained Tom.

"No sign of Dungly or Morgana," said Jack.

"Nor Starlight," sighed Tom. "It looks like we were wrong."

Jade studied the ruins intently. "No," she replied excitedly. "I think I can see him."

**Can you find Starlight?**

# Prisoners!

We'd better move the unicorn. These meddling children might have told others where it is.

It still looks sick. Put it on your cart along with my horse — I exhausted it riding here.

Then lock these three in the dungeon!

And so...

Whew! It's stuffy in here.

At least there's a gap under the door, so we have some air.

How can they escape?

# On the right track

They quickly scrambled from the dungeon — but there was no sign of Morgana, Dungly or Starlight.

"We're back where we started," sighed Tom. "They could have gone anywhere."

"Don't give up," said Jade, climbing on her horse. "We may still catch them."

As they rode along, the earth beneath their horses' hooves became softer.

"Hey, look!" said Jade, pointing at the ground ahead, "Tracks! But which ones are Dungly's horse and cart?"

Jack thought back to something he'd read earlier. "I know which ones to follow," he cried. "Let's go!"

**Which tracks should they follow?**

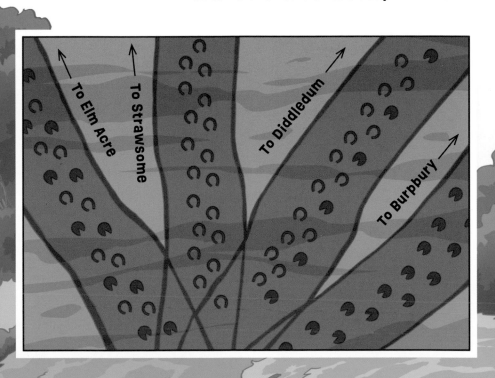

# The unicorn parade

The three friends arrive at Diddledum...

There's Dungly's cart!

They jump off their horses and Tom leaps in front of the cart...

**Out of our way**, boy!

What's going on here?

I'm the king's sister and I **demand** you let me pass!

Princess Morgana **stole** the king's unicorn. Look!

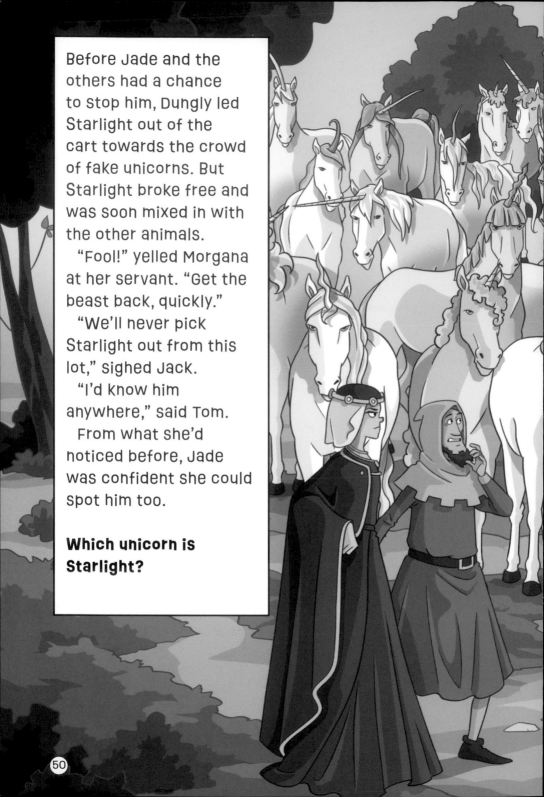

Before Jade and the others had a chance to stop him, Dungly led Starlight out of the cart towards the crowd of fake unicorns. But Starlight broke free and was soon mixed in with the other animals.

"Fool!" yelled Morgana at her servant. "Get the beast back, quickly."

"We'll never pick Starlight out from this lot," sighed Jack.

"I'd know him anywhere," said Tom.

From what she'd noticed before, Jade was confident she could spot him too.

**Which unicorn is Starlight?**

# Punt problem

Tom flung himself onto Starlight's back. "Climb up, quickly!" he yelled to Jade and Jack.

With Leo clutched in Jade's arms, the three friends held tight, as Tom urged Starlight into action.

"Come back, you little toads!" screamed Morgana, as they galloped past, out of the village.

"We'll come back for our horses later," cried Tom. "We must get Starlight to the king before Morgana catches us. I'll take the fastest route from here, between Elm Acre and Birch Hill."

"Oh no!" said Jade, when they reached the river. "The bridge is broken!"

BRIDGE
UNSAFE!

Not far away was a large punt next to a sign.

"Someone will need to cross with Starlight," said Tom, "and then stay with him once he's across."

"We'll have to take the punt back each time," sighed Jade. "And Morgana is hot on our heels."

Jack thought for a moment. "It's okay," he said. "We can all get across quite quickly, if we plan it."

**What is the minimum number of crossings needed to get everyone across?**

Peter Puddle's Punts Ltd.

Price: 1 groat per crossing

Max. weight per crossing:
2 persons
or
1 person + 1 horse
(small dogs may cross at any time)

GONE TO
YE LUNCH

# A surprise confession

**What is Jade's plan?**

# Unicorn magic

Can you translate Moglin's spell?

# A final feast

King Edgar is surrounded by a magical swirl...

Whooosh!

Cool!

Wow!

WOOF!

Once Tom has introduced his friends...

We owe you our gratitude. I hereby proclaim you Lord Jack and Lady Jade.

Thank you, Your Majesty!

WOOF!

As the king leads everyone inside...

You must join us for the feast!

Sit them at the top table, Tom, according to the rules of court.

**Seating plan**

| Sir Greave | Baroness Vole | Baron Beef | Baroness Beef | King Edgar | Princess Morgana | Moglin | Baroness Flint | Sir Osric |
| --- | --- | --- | --- | --- | --- | --- | --- | --- |

Top table

Spare seat | Side table | Side table | Spare seat

Here's the seating plan from the last feast. The rules are on the back.

### Court seating rules

-Only Barons and Baronesses may sit next to the King, with the exception of Queens, Princes and Princesses.

-Barons and Baronesses must sit nearer to the King than Knights (Knights are those with the title Sir).

-Lords and Ladies may not sit nearer to the King than Barons and Baronesses. But they must sit nearer than Knights.

-No two men must sit next to each other at the top table.

-Moglin must sit to the King's left, one place removed.

(You may move people around from their current positions on the seating plan if necessary.)

**Where should Jade and Jack sit, moving the fewest people possible?**

# Going home

# Return to the future

**M**oments later, Jade, Jack and Leo were back in the shed, dressed in their normal clothes.

"We're home!" gasped Jack, happy to be back in familiar surroundings. "But my parents are going to be mad," he added, nervously. "How do I explain where I've been all this time?"

"I don't think you'll need to worry about that," Jade said, holding up her phone which had returned to her pocket.

"Exactly the same time and date we left!" said Jack.

"Maybe that's how time travel works," Jade replied.

King Edgar
Reign: 1345-1395

REMINDER
-DO NOT TOUCH UNLESS
PREPARED TO TRAVEL!

Queen Victoria
Born: 1819
Died: 1901

Jack looked thoughtful. "Do you think we *really* **did** travel back in time?" he asked. "Now we're home, that stuff with the unicorn feels like some kind of dream."

"We can't have had the same dream," said Jade. She glanced at her aunt's collection for some sort of explanation.

Then she noticed something that hadn't been there when they left. "I think I can prove we went back in time," she said. "And not only that, it shows we changed history for the better!"

**What has Jade spotted?**

# Clues

**Page 6**
What object has Jade seen on page 5 that has writing on it?

**Page 7**
Look at the sign above the shed door. Try saying the words out loud like Jack.

**Page 9**
Look at the dates on the picture of Queen Victoria.

**Page 12**
Look at the plants in the picture. Then read the information in the Book of Unicorns.

**Page 15**
As Jade says, try reading the message from top to bottom instead of left to right.

**Page 19**
There's something hidden in the picture which explains why Tom fell asleep.

**Page 21**
Just follow Tom's directions carefully.

**Page 25**
Look at the time of day in each vision and keep an eye out for the potion bottle.

**Page 27**
Which object can Jade use as a mirror?

**Page 29**
Put the pieces of the note back together like a jigsaw puzzle.

**Page 32**
Look at page 31 for a reminder of what boggleberries look like.

**Page 35**
Eliminate the horses that are lame, being shod or have never been ridden (plus one is only suitable for Jade).

**Page 37**
Morgana must be going to a place close to the village Dungly mentioned in his note to her. Unlike Morgana, Jack and the others can take a shortcut that goes through any village.

## Page 39

Tom's description of Dungly only matches one of the villager's descriptions of him exactly.

## Page 41

Look out for Starlight's horn, as featured in the picture on page 13. Only one horn is real.

## Page 45

They have a sheet of paper (Morgana's map) and a long, thin metal poker. There is also a slight gap under the door. Together, these things can help Jade free the key from the lock.

## Page 47

See Dungly's note on page 29 for information about his horse.

## Page 50

Only one unicorn in the parade exactly matches the picture of Starlight you've seen earlier.

## Page 53

If two people cross first and one of them returns, you should be able to work out the remaining crossings.

## Page 57

What has Morgana previously written which proves she ordered Dungly to steal the unicorn?

## Page 61

Every word in the spell is in English, the letters just need rearranging.

## Page 65

Morgana will now be missing from the feast.

Jack and Jade have just been made a lord and a lady.

Remember you can use the spare seats if necessary.

## Page 67

Look back at the note from Auntie Blossom that Jade found in the Book of Unicorns.

## Page 69

One of the objects has been replaced with something similar.

# Answers

## Page 6

Jade noticed that Jack's name is written on his soccer ball (see page 5).

## Page 7

Some or parts of the words in the sign above the door are homophones. This means that they sound the same as other words. In this case:

-**for**get = four
-**to** = two
-g**ate** = eight

So the combination of the lock is 4, 2, 8.

## Page 9

The photograph shows Auntie Blossom with Queen Victoria. There is another picture of the Queen amongst Blossom's collection of objects. That picture says Victoria died in 1901. If Blossom was around 30 when she met Victoria, she'd be over 150 years old now. That would be impossible.

## Page 12

The description of the Greenwood Unicorn mentions that Greenwood Forest is the only place in the land where blue-leafed clovers grow. Jade, Jack and Leo are surrounded by these plants, so Jade realizes they must be in Greenwood Forest.

## Page 15

Reading only the first word of each line reveals a hidden message:

*Take the unicorn at midnight all is prepared*

## Page 19

Jade has seen a bottle of sleeping potion in the stable. She realizes someone probably put the potion in Tom's drink which is why he fell asleep.

## Page 21

This is the door to Moglin's chamber.

route →

## Page 25

In the vision at sunrise, during Sir Osric's visit, the potion bottle is still visible as Osric leaves the room.

In the vision at midday, the bottle has gone. So it must have been taken by Morgana during her visit. You can just see it poking out from her robes.

The bottle is still missing when Sir Greave visits Moglin at sunset.

potion bottle

sunrise          midday          sunset

## Page 27

Jade can use the reflective surface of the knight's helmet as a mirror to read the note. Here's what it says the right way around...

Time Travel Notes

– some objects have time energy

– this energy can transport you through time

– the object can return you to your own time...

...but <u>only</u> after a task connected with the object has been completed!

## Page 29

Once the torn parts of the note are put back together, the message from Dungly to Morgana reads as follows...

Dear Princess Morgana,

I hope you're well. Sorry to bother you, but the unicorn doesn't look too good. Its legs have gone wobbly and it won't stop shivering. I went to the nearest village for advice (I didn't mention the stolen unicorn, obviously).
A man in the Groggle Inn said it sounded like a case of Fettle Fever. He said the only cure is boggleberry juice. The village shop was right out of boggleberries, so I asked a lad there to take this message to you. Any chance you could bring some boggleberries as soon as possible? Hoping this finds you as it leaves me.

Your obedient and crawly servant,

Dungly

P.S. My cart horse has lost its back right shoe. If you see it lying around on your way over, let me know.

## Page 32

Here is the boggleberry seller.                          Morgana

## Page 35

Of the six horses, Samson, the large chestnut (brown) horse, is lame; Dotty is still being shod by the blacksmith and Molly, the silver dappled horse, has never been ridden, so is unsafe to ride. That only leaves Lightning, Snowflake and Valiant. Jade will have to ride Snowflake, as that horse only likes female riders.

---

## Page 37

In his letter to Morgana, Dungly said that he visited the nearest village of Groggle. So he must be keeping Starlight somewhere near there.

Morgana's route

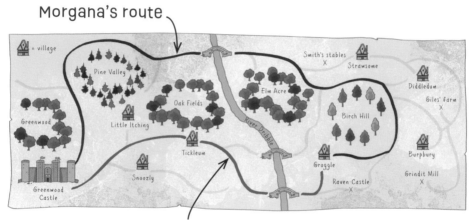

Tom, Jack and Jade's route

---

## Page 39

Tom says Dungly has a brown beard, isn't tall and has no hair on his head. Only the description given by the villager pictured on the right matches all those things. Therefore Dungly was going to Raven Castle.

## Page 41

The top of Starlight's horn is circled in yellow. The other horns in the picture are broken parts of statues and are too low to be Starlight.

## Page 45

Jade can slip Morgana's map under the door. By putting the long metal poker into the keyhole, she can then push the key out of the lock, so that it falls onto the map. She can then pull the map and the key inside the dungeon.

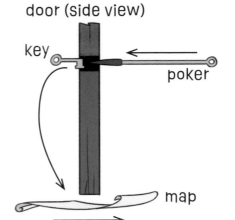

door (side view)

key

poker

map

## Page 47

In Dungly's letter to Morgana, he said that his horse had lost its back right shoe. So the tracks that show three horseshoe prints and one back right hoofprint must belong to Dungly's horse.

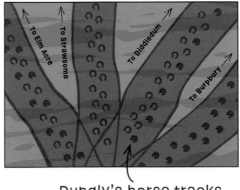

To Elm Acre

To Strawsome

To Diddledum

To Burpbury

Dungly's horse tracks

## Page 50

If you compare the picture of Starlight on page 13 with the unicorns in the parade, only the one circled in yellow matches.

## Page 53

On the first crossing, two people will need to go across. One will then stay on the far bank while the other returns the punt to the beginning, where they will pick up Starlight and cross again. Having left Starlight on the far bank, that person then returns to collect the third person and they cross together. This makes a total of five crossings. Leo can cross at any time.

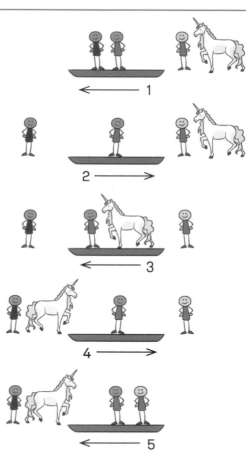

## Page 57

Jade wants Morgana to write something so that she can prove that the handwriting matches that on the note (seen on page 15) which ordered Dungly to steal the unicorn.

## Page 61

Moglin's spell is just English backwards. He says:

*Oh mystic beast, with horn so white, please hear my magic spell...restore our good king back to health, so he might rule us well.*

## Page 65

Morgana will be missing from the feast. So Baroness Flint will move up two places to take her place. Jade will take Baroness Flint's place.

Jack will take Sir Greave's place. Sir Greave will move along one to take the spare seat.

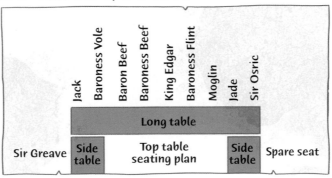

## Page 67

The note that Jade found inside the Book of Unicorns told her that the book would return them home once a task connected to it had been completed.

## Page 69

The painting of Queen Morgana has been replaced by one of King Edgar. Morgana's painting indicated she was queen from 1375, the year she stole the unicorn. The painting of Edgar states he was king from 1345 to 1395. As Jade and Jack stopped Morgana's plan, it meant she never became queen. This would explain why her painting was replaced — history was correcting itself!

# If you enjoyed this story, keep a look out for more puzzling time travel adventures with Jade, Jack and Leo!

## Edited by Lesley Sims

First published in 2023 by Usborne Publishing Limited, 83-85 Saffron Hill, London EC1N 8RT, United Kingdom. usborne.com Copyright © 2023 Usborne Publishing Limited. The name Usborne and the Balloon logo are registered trade marks of Usborne Publishing Limited. All rights reserved. No part of this publication may be reproduced, stored in a retrieval system or transmitted in any form or by any means without prior permission of the publisher. UE. First published in America in 2023. This edition first published in America in 2024.